I let them have it.

'I'm going to be working on the disappearance of
Smith and Wesson,' I said. 'You know, the
notorious bank robbers who were last seen in this
area before they vanished without trace . . .'

I heard several sharp intakes of adult breath
around me. Mr Pinkerton's face was a picture, I'm
glad to say. As I spoke, his grin slowly froze, and
he closed his eyes in horror. Sir Nicholas just
looked very cross.

'So *that's* what you're up to,' said Sergeant Cuff. I'd
forgotten he was there. 'I should have known.'

I suddenly realized I'd said too much in front of
him. I was cross with myself. I'd been so eager to
have some fun at Mr Pinkerton's expense I'd given
the game away. Now Sergeant Cuff knew the real
purpose of my stay at Courtenay House, and he
didn't like it. Not one little bit . . .

*Sam, the Girl Detective: The Secret of the Seventh
Candle* is the fourth title in a series of hilarious
mysteries starring Sam Marlowe, intrepid girl
detective.

Sam, the Girl Detective:
The Secret of the Seventh Candle

TONY BRADMAN

Illustrated by Doffy Weir

YEARLING

SAM, THE GIRL DETECTIVE:
THE SECRET OF THE SEVENTH CANDLE

A YEARLING BOOK 0 440 86309 0

First publication in Great Britain

PRINTING HISTORY
Yearling edition published 1992

Text copyright © 1992 by Tony Bradman
Illustrations copyright © 1992 by Doffy Weir

This book is set in 14/16pt Century Schoolbook
by Kestrel Data, Exeter

Yearling Books are published by Transworld Publishers Ltd.,
61-63 Uxbridge Road, Ealing, London W5 5SA, in Australia by
Transworld Publishers (Australia) Pty. Ltd., 15-23 Helles
Avenue, Moorebank, NSW 2170, and in New Zealand by
Transworld Publishers (N.Z.) Ltd., 3 William Pickering Drive,
Albany, Auckland.

Made and printed in Great Britain by
Cox & Wyman Ltd, Reading, Berks.

For all the Seymours –
but especially Nicola

Chapter One

It was one of those baking hot afternoons in the summer term when your brain feels like melted cheese, and you could kill for a tall glass of something cool and refreshing. Heck, I would have happily slaughtered the whole of Class Nine for a single, solitary ice cube.

I wasn't going to get one though, whatever I did. The world might think of me as Sam Marlowe, intrepid girl detective. But as far as Chandler Street Junior was concerned, I was just another schoolkid. Which meant I would be trapped at my desk for a while yet, with no relief in sight.

'Right, everyone,' said my teacher,

Mrs Sternwood. 'I want you to turn to the map on page seven . . .'

There were groans and the rustling of paper as the class did what it was told. It was a Geography lesson, and I was sharing a book with my friend, Richard Watson.

I tried hard to listen to what Mrs Sternwood was saying. But my mind had wandered before she'd finished her first sentence, even though it's a subject I enjoy. After all, you can never tell when a skill like map-reading could come in useful.

The fly buzzing round my head might have agreed.

He'd flown in with a pal when I'd opened the window earlier, but the friendship hadn't lasted. The chum had developed engine trouble, taken a nosedive and crash landed. He was lying on my ruler with his legs in the air.

I didn't need to be a genius at biology to realize his next stop had been Insect Heaven. Maybe he'd get a better set of wings there. But The

Case of the Dead Fly was open and shut. I was sure the poor, dumb bug had died of heat exhaustion and thirst. I was beginning to wonder if I might be next.

And now the first one couldn't find the way out. Every so often he'd collide with his own reflection in the window. I took pity on him, and opened it a little wider. He didn't stop to say thanks. But a detective gets used to that.

'*Samantha Marlowe!*' Mrs Sternwood shouted suddenly. I almost jumped out of my skin. 'I don't think you've heard a single word I've said. Leave that window alone, and pay attention!'

'Please, miss,' said someone at the back of the class. 'She's been fiddling with it all through the lesson.'

I knew who that was without even looking. The whining voice belonged to Class Nine's biggest creep, Steven Greenstreet. He's my deadliest enemy, and he's always trying to get me into trouble. He's got a gang with four of his mates, but they're so pathetic I call them The Feeble Five.

'I was just trying to stop myself passing out, Miss,' I said. 'I don't think I can stand the smell much longer.'

The class cracked up. The laugh was on Greenstreet. To be precise, it was on the huge, ghastly trainers he wore all the time. Trainers make your feet sweat a lot, even in cold weather. In the heat we'd been having they can be lethal. And that's exactly what Greenstreet's were.

The warm weather had started on Monday, and by the end of the week, an awful pong was coming from under Greenstreet's desk. It was why Mrs Sternwood had moved him to the back of the class. She said she couldn't think properly if he was any closer. The rest of us kept as far away from him as possible.

I'd made Greenstreet's feet a running joke, though.

Every time I saw him in the playground I held my nose, and said in a robot voice: 'Warning! Warning! Toxic Toe Alert! E-vac-u-ate! E-vac-u-ate!' That morning I'd told him he should be hearing from *Friends of the Earth* any day. After all, he *was* a major threat to our environment.

Judging by the look of pure hate he was giving me with his piggy eyes, Greenstreet was thinking of making a threat of another kind. To my health, probably. But he didn't worry me. I could tackle him with one arm tied behind my back. Although I would *definitely* need a gas mask . . .

'I'll get you for that, Marlowe,' he was spluttering.

'Put a sock in it, Greenstreet,' I drawled, grinning as the class roared. I paused, then went for the knockout. 'And make it a *clean* one.'

Greenstreet stood up, pushing his chair over backwards. But he didn't get very far. Mrs Sternwood fixed him with one of her special, withering stares and told him to sit down *im-mediately*. He did . . . only he'd forgotten his chair wasn't there, and

fell on his rear end with a bump. Everyone howled.

'Stop playing the fool, Steven, and sort yourself out,' said Mrs Sternwood crossly. She dabbed at her forehead with a small handkerchief. 'And be quiet, the rest of you. I *do* hope you'll be better behaved than this on the school journey. After last year's performance you're lucky to be going at all.'

We'd been treated to a lot of comments like that recently. It's only to be expected, I suppose. The teachers seem to dread the prospect of the school journey, but they still take the two top classes on one every summer term. Strange people, teachers. Sometimes I'm convinced I'll never understand them.

I mean, they even have some crazy idea the whole thing should be educational. You'd think they'd have realized by now most kids simply see it as an opportunity to get away from home and go completely wild for a week. That's what my classmates had done last time, at any rate.

We'd stayed at a hotel. The teachers took us on loads of long hikes to places they said would be interesting. But as you can imagine, they turned out to be *very* boring. So both classes made up for it with wild games, practical jokes and midnight feasts. Not me, though. I kept pretty much to myself.

Of course, Mrs Sternwood and the other teachers hadn't been very happy about what went on. In fact, they'd spent the entire week shouting. When we left, there was even a rumour the hotel manager had suffered a nervous breakdown. It might have been true. He did ban the school from ever coming back.

That was fine by me. I had good reason to be pleased we were visiting somewhere else this year — a *very* good reason indeed. We were heading for a campsite in the grounds of Courtenay House, a well known stately home. The nearest town went by the name of Stembridge.

It was a place I knew a lot about already.

'And that reminds me,' continued Mrs Sternwood, 'I seem to remember saying you had until today to decide on the themes for your school journey projects. Hands up those who've done as I asked . . .'

This was a new wheeze, although like all our teachers' schemes, it was about as subtle as a brick through a window, and ten times more obvious. It was the old keep-'em-busy-and-they-won't-cause-trouble trick, but with a difference. This year they were actually offering a *prize* for the best project.

They weren't saying what the prize was, though, and I didn't think it would be wonderful. Our headmaster, Mr Pinkerton, is always complaining about how little money the school's got. Mind you, I had to give the teachers credit; if this was a con, it was a beauty. Everyone in the class had their hands up.

Richard was doing a terrific impersonation of a drowning man. He kept hissing 'Miss! Miss!' too. For a second I thought he was going to burst. He didn't. But when Mrs Sternwood finally let him speak, he burbled on and on about the history of the Stembridge area. He seemed to have done his project already.

'And what have *you* got planned, Samantha?' said Mrs Sternwood once she'd shut him up. She gave me her encouraging smile. 'Something historical too, perhaps?'

'Not exactly, Miss . . .' I said.

No, I'd come up with something a *lot* more interesting.

I calmly announced I wanted to do a project on Smith and Wesson, alias 'The Lucky Number Bandits'. They were a notorious duo of bank robbers who'd made fun of the police for not being able to catch them. Then they'd mysteriously disappeared, just over five months ago.

And the last place they'd been spotted was . . . Stembridge.

All the newspapers had covered the case, and there had even been a couple of programmes on TV about it. But no-one had found a trace of the pair yet. They seemed to have vanished into thin air. It was a mystery waiting to be solved, and I knew only one person capable of doing it. Me.

I could see the headline now: *Brilliant Girl Detective Tracks Down Missing Villains, Finds Loot*. Now there's something to put in your scrapbook . . .

'That wasn't really the sort of thing I had in mind, Samantha,' Mrs Sternwood said. She had a pained expression on her face. 'I'm sure it's very interesting, but . . .'

I'd heard that 'but' from grown-ups before. It meant I'd have to do some fast talking to save my project idea — but that's something I've always been good at. Mrs Sternwood came round to liking it in the end. At least, I *think* she did . . .

When the lesson was over, Richard and I walked out of the classroom and headed for the drinking fountain. I thought Greenstreet and his gang might have followed us, but they didn't. Instead, they huddled together muttering, and gave us several dirty looks.

I added a couple of tons of mud and gave the looks back.

They were *very* predictable. I knew they would want to try pulling a few strokes on me during the school journey. They might even be starting to work out some tricks already.

That's OK, I thought, and smiled.

So was I.

Chapter Two

'Now are you *sure* you've got enough underwear?' said Dad, loudly. 'I know you, Sam Marlowe. You've probably packed more detective stories in that rucksack than clean knickers.'

'*Dad!*' I hissed. 'Keep your voice down.'

Few children realize parents are specially trained to embarrass their offspring. They go to a top-secret college where they learn how to reduce you to a stuttering, blushing wreck. Lesson One is: 'Incredibly Embarrassing Things To Say When Your Daughter Is Surrounded By Her Classmates.'

It was a hot, sunny, Saturday

morning, and we were waiting outside the school gates for a coach to arrive. When it did, the driver would load up our luggage and we would set off for Stembridge. All I had to do was survive the next few minutes without completely losing my reputation.

I glanced over my shoulder. Luckily, no-one seemed to have heard. It occurred to me that the others were far too busy being embarrassed by their own parents to listen to mine. There were plenty of them around, too, adults of every shape and size, many of them dead ringers for their kids.

For instance, Richard and his dad are identical. With their thin legs and thick glasses, they're more like twins than father and son. And Greenstreet is such a copy of his mum it's eerie. I didn't know which one to feel sorry for the most.

'Here's the coach now,' said *my* mum as it came round the corner. 'Philip, help your little sister with her things.'

That 'little' nearly made me blow my top, but I decided it wasn't worth it. Sometimes I wonder if my mother wants me ever to grow up. Then again, maybe she does, and she's just keeping me on my toes by putting Lesson Two into operation – that's the one called: 'How To Treat Your Daughter Like A Baby In Public.'

'Don't worry, Mum,' I said, snatching my rucksack and sleeping bag from my big brother, who was smirking. 'I think I can *just* about manage.'

I went over to the coach, where the teachers were attempting to get things organized. There were at least half a dozen of them acting as our minders on this trip, including Mrs Patel, the deputy head, and Mrs Sternwood. I thought Mrs Sternwood looked very cool and casual in her pressed Bermuda shorts and neat T-shirt.

Mr Pinkerton wasn't wearing his usual frayed, ink-stained jacket and baggy, wrinkled trousers. He'd replaced them with a shiny shell suit that came in a dazzling combination of pink, green and orange. He reminded me of an ice cream I'd once had. It had dripped a lot. Mr Pinkerton seemed to be melting, too.

'Get back, you horrible lot!' he was saying. His bald skull and bushy eyebrows were damp with perspiration. The latter looked like two miniature rain forests. 'How many times do I have to tell you not to push and shove? It won't help us get there any more quickly, you know.'

Like the other teachers, Mr Pinkerton looked as if he wished the school journey was over, rather than just beginning. I could hardly blame him. Everyone was trying to give their bags and cases to the driver at once, and the headmaster was caught in the middle. It all took a lot longer than it should have done.

But at last the driver slammed the boot door, and we were ready to roll.

Richard had saved me a place, so I didn't have to get involved in any of

'Touch that and you die, Marlowe'

the nasty disagreements over seating that were going on around us. The Feeble Five were leaning heavily on some kids to give them the back row. In the struggle a zip-up bag was kicked along the aisle. I leant down to pick it up.

'Touch that and you *die*, Marlowe,'

yelled Greenstreet. He came lurching towards me, murder in his eyes.

'Thanks for the warning, Greenstreet,' I said. 'I didn't realize you had another pair of trainers in it.'

Richard and I burst out laughing, but Greenstreet didn't seem to enjoy the gag. He's never had much of a sense of humour. Not as far as *my* jokes are concerned, that is.

'Just you stay away from my stuff,' he said, doing his best to sound menacing. He grabbed the bag and scurried off, holding it protectively under one arm.

It was an odd incident. Greenstreet had seemed pretty worried about the possibility of me handling his bag. I know I'm not his favourite person, but even so, his reaction had roused my suspicions. But perhaps it didn't mean that much.

I shrugged, and looked out of the window. My family were lined up on the pavement, waving. Dad always gets sentimental on occasions like this, so I wasn't surprised to see he was a bit tearful. Mum was mouthing 'Send us a postcard!', and my wonderful brother was sticking his tongue out. Charming.

I love my family, I really do. But I don't mind telling you I was glad to be having some time away from them.

Pity it was only a week, I thought, smiling and waving as the driver revved the engine and the coach moved off . . .

We hadn't been going long when Richard suddenly got very agitated. He knelt on his seat and looked up and down the coach. He seemed to be searching for someone.

'What's wrong, Richard?' I said. He took no notice.

'Miss! Miss!' he shouted. 'Stop the coach!'

'I'm sorry, Richard,' said Mrs Sternwood when she came down the aisle, 'but you should have gone before we left school. You'll have to wait until our first scheduled halt . . .'

'It's not that, Miss,' said Richard, urgently. 'I think we've left Mr Pinkerton behind!'

Richard's OK, but he can be a real goody-goody sometimes. He was right, of course. I did my own quick seat check, and soon saw Mr Pinkerton definitely wasn't on board. Personally, I didn't think that was a problem, and couldn't understand why Richard was making such a fuss.

If anyone had asked me, I'd have said the school journey would probably be better *without* our wonderful headmaster. And from some of the things others nearby were whispering, I reckoned they agreed. Richard heard them too, and realized what he'd done. A look of shame slowly crept over his face.

He didn't have to worry. It turned out there had never been any chance of us escaping Mr Pinkerton.

'How very observant of you, Richard,' said Mrs Sternwood through tight lips. 'But there's no need for alarm. We haven't abandoned the

26

headmaster. He isn't on the coach with us because he decided to drive to Stembridge in his car. It's all right for some, that's what I say.'

Mrs Sternwood had mumbled the last part, but I'd heard it well enough. She was obviously pretty cheesed off Mr Pinkerton wasn't sharing the coach journey with her and the other teachers. It was easy to see why. I didn't particularly want to spend three hours on a coach with this lot myself.

You know how it is. There's always someone who gets travel-sick and dumps their breakfast on the lap of the person next to them. There are fights, and kids screaming, and teachers shouting. There are constant stops so everyone can go to the toilet. And there's usually a traffic jam, too.

All that happened on the way to Stembridge, and more.

As the day wore on, it got hotter, and hotter. *Three* kids were spectacularly sick. Then the driver threatened to take us back to Chandler Street because there was so much arguing. And that was just between the teachers. None of them wanted to do any clearing up. Mrs Sternwood got the job in the end.

Meanwhile, Mr Pinkerton pottered along behind us in his brand new car, the one he'd bought a few weeks ago and was so proud of. To me, cars are simply metal boxes on wheels that knock people over and cause pollution. But Mr Pinkerton adores them, and this one was the greatest love of his life.

At school he kept it parked right outside his study window. He seemed to spend half his day running out to bellow at anyone who even looked at it. The penalty for damaging this amazing machine was probably death, or something even more cruel, like maths homework every night for the rest of your life.

It was lunchtime when we arrived. As it was Saturday, Stembridge High Street was crowded, which gave

Greenstreet and his gang an opportunity to make faces at everyone we passed. But I blocked The Feeble Five out of my mind. I concentrated on checking out a place I knew only from the TV and the papers.

It pretty much matched the pictures I'd seen and the descriptions I'd read. There was the Town Hall and the War Memorial, the Post Office and the market square. Soon we were in open fields again, heading for the campsite.

We went past an old church, round a bend . . . and there on top of a hill was Courtenay House. It was bigger than a garden shed, and smaller than Buckingham Palace, but only just. It had a curved, gravel drive, and so many towers and turrets I expected to see Count Dracula waiting for us on the doorstep.

Instead, there was a tall, elderly man with the biggest ears I'd seen outside the elephant enclosure at the zoo. He was standing with a couple of other people. One was a tiny, dark-

haired woman . . . and the other, a large policeman. His car was parked in the road outside the gate, beside a tree.

We all piled out of the coach, and the driver started to unload our luggage. Then Mrs Sternwood called my name. I turned round, and saw she was talking to the policeman. She didn't seem too cheerful. In fact, if her eyes had been lasers, I would have been instantly converted into a puff of black smoke.

'This is Sergeant Cuff, Samantha,' she said. 'Apparently he was here to talk about security at Courtenay House, but now he says he'd like to have a word with you. I can't imagine why . . . I just *hope* this doesn't mean you're in some kind of trouble already.'

I looked up at Sergeant Cuff's steely blue eyes.

That makes two of us, I thought.

Chapter Three

'I wonder if I might chat with Samantha alone, Mrs Sternwood?' said Sergeant Cuff. His voice was quiet and slow, and he had a strong country accent. 'I think it would be the best idea . . .'

'Oh . . . I suppose it's all right,' she said. 'So long as you can assure me I *will* find out what this is about?'

Sergeant Cuff didn't reply. He simply gave Mrs Sternwood a sketchy salute, then gripped my elbow and gently guided me out of hearing range. I was still close enough to feel a ten thousand megawatt teacher-glare burning into my back, though. Maybe she *did* have laser eyes.

She wasn't the only one watching, either. The Chandler Street kids were gawping, of course, but so were Mr Big-Ears and The Little Lady. Both of them were staring as if I'd been caught stealing the family silver. Someone else had appeared too, a youngish guy in a black jacket with tails.

Maybe I should sell tickets, I thought.

'So you're the famous Sam Marlowe,' said Sergeant Cuff. 'I must say you're a bit of a disappointment.'

'Oh yeah?' I said. 'What were you expecting?'

'Not a skinny schoolgirl,' he said. 'A mean-looking private detective, maybe. About six feet tall, with a nasty scar and a gun. At least, that's the picture I had in my mind after I'd talked to . . . Inspector Raven.'

So that was it. My old partner in crime had been beating the jungle drums. Inspector Raven and I have worked on a lot of cases together. Correction. I've worked on them, and he's done nothing but interfere. I should have known he'd warn the Stembridge law I was on my way.

'I didn't realize he was keeping such close tabs on me,' I said. 'Where did he get the information? Is my phone tapped?'

'Nothing so complicated,' said Sergeant Cuff with a smile. 'There was a story in your local paper about a certain upcoming school journey. Inspector Raven read it, then gave me a call. I had to pay Courtenay House a visit anyway, so I thought I'd use the opportunity to check you out. But you don't look like much trouble to me.'

'Nice of you to say so,' I said, and smiled back.

I was beginning to warm to this big man. I liked his voice, and his eyes weren't really steely. They had more of a twinkle. It turned out he had a daughter my age, and pretty soon he and I were getting on fine. He reminded me of my dad. I don't know why. They're as different as chalk and cheese.

'I think I'd better put your teacher

out of her misery,' he said at last. 'By the look of her she thinks I'm about to arrest you. Just remember, though,' he said, suddenly serious, 'that's *exactly* what I will do if you give me any bother. I've got too much on my plate as it is. Understand?'

'You bet, Sarge,' I said, cranking up my deluxe 'angelic schoolgirl' smile to as wide as it would go. 'I'll be as good as gold, cross my heart. So long as you promise not to mention Inspector Raven, that is. Do we have a deal?'

'We do,' said Sergeant Cuff, and laughed.

I laughed too as we walked back to the others, but for a different reason. Sergeant Cuff had done his best to warn me off. What he didn't know was that I'd already filed his warning with the others I've had in the past – under 'I' for 'Ignore', if you hadn't guessed.

A grim-faced Mrs Sternwood had been joined by Mrs Patel, who looked like she was sucking a lemon. Mr Pinkerton had arrived, so with Mr Big-Ears, the Little Lady and the guy in the tailcoat, there was a large group of grown-ups waiting for an explanation. I was hoping Sergeant Cuff had a good one.

He did.

'Well?' said Mrs Sternwood. 'What's she done, Sergeant?'

'Nothing at all,' said Sergeant Cuff. 'There's no reason to be concerned. I was simply saying hello. We have a, er . . . mutual friend who let me know she was coming . . .'

That was one way of putting it, I suppose. For a second I didn't think the sergeant was going to pull it off. Mrs Sternwood gave him the look she uses when she isn't buying one of my wilder excuses for being late. But then Mr Big-Ears stepped in and saved my bacon.

'I say, that *is* a relief, Sergeant,' he said. 'One was rather concerned for a moment. There's certainly no room for any juvenile delinquents *here*.'

'Quite,' said the Little Lady.

'And you can rest assured that we haven't brought any with us, Sir

Nicholas,' said Mr Pinkerton hastily. He put one hand over his heart. 'I can honestly and categorically state that anything bad you might have heard about Chandler Street School is *completely* untrue . . .'

Thanks to our headmaster, I now knew the real identity of Mr Big-Ears. He was Sir Nicholas Courtenay, the man who owned Courtenay House, and the Little Lady must have been his wife, Lady Jennifer. No wonder Mr Pinkerton was being so polite.

We'd been told all about them of course, real aristocrats who had opened their house to the public and ran a campsite for school parties. It was interesting to see them in the flesh. They didn't seem any different from ordinary people.

'Sarah here is one of our brightest pupils,' said Mr Pinkerton, patting my shoulder. He gets most people's names wrong, unless he thinks they're important, that is, like Sir Nicholas. 'And weren't you telling me she'd come up with a very interesting idea for a project, Mrs Stevens?'

'Er . . . yes, that's right,' said Mrs Sternwood, nervously. 'But I'm not sure whether Sir Nicholas . . .'

I could see her mind racing. For a teacher, Mrs Sternwood can be very clever. And she was obviously thinking that someone who was worried by juvenile delinquents might not want to hear I was doing a project about criminals. She did her best to stop Mr Pinkerton, but he insisted I reveal all.

So I let them have it.

'I'm going to be working on the disappearance of Smith and Wesson,' I said. 'You know, the notorious bank robbers who were last seen in this area before they vanished without trace . . .'

I heard several sharp intakes of adult breath around me. Mr Pinkerton's face was a picture, I'm glad to say. As I spoke, his grin slowly froze, and he closed his eyes in horror. Sir Nicholas just looked very cross.

'Good Lord!' he said. 'One hardly

thinks such a subject is appropriate
for a child of your tender years.'

'Quite,' said Lady Jennifer.

'Actually, Sir Nicholas, I was hoping I could ask you a few questions,' I
said. 'I believe there was evidence of
some connection between Courtenay
House and the bandits.'

'Absolutely impossible,' said Sir
Nicholas briskly, his nostrils flaring,

one eyebrow shooting skywards. 'Wherever could you have heard such an *outrageous* suggestion?'

'It was in several of the newspaper reports,' I said. 'The robbers were spotted in a car near your gate . . .'

'That is simply untrue,' said Sir Nicholas. He was giving me the snootiest look I've ever seen in my life. 'And one has no further comment to make on this particular matter. Is that perfectly clear, young lady?'

'Quite,' I said, before Lady Jennifer could.

I couldn't resist it, although I wished I'd kept my mouth shut as soon as the word slipped out. Mr Pinkerton groaned, and I didn't dare look at Mrs Sternwood. But I could have sworn Sergeant Cuff was trying to stop himself laughing. Mr Tailcoat had an odd expression on his face, too.

'I think perhaps we ought to get the children settled in,' said Mrs Sternwood. 'Could someone show us to the campsite?'

'By all means,' said Sir Nicholas

grumpily. 'My butler Walters will take you there now.'

He turned on his heel and strode off through the massive double doors, with Lady Jennifer tagging along behind him. Somehow I didn't think either of them would be signing up for my fan club just yet. Oh well, I thought. If I'd wanted to be popular I should never have become a detective.

At least I could be grateful I wasn't their butler. It was easy to see Sir Nicholas loved telling people what to do. And if there's one thing I'd *never* win a prize for, it's taking orders. Walters was the guy in the fancy jacket, and he bustled off along a path that led round the side of the house.

'This way, please!' he called out.

I had the distinct impression Mr Pinkerton wanted to say something to me, but he didn't get the chance. Everyone started following Walters with their luggage, and the headmaster was swept away. Within seconds the only visible part of him was his bald pate. It shone brightly in the sunlight.

'So *that's* what you're up to,' said Sergeant Cuff. I'd forgotten he was there. 'I should have known . . .'

I suddenly realized I'd said too much in front of him. I was cross with myself. I'd been so eager to have some fun at Mr Pinkerton's expense I'd given the game away. Now Sergeant Cuff knew the real purpose of my stay at Courtenay House, and he didn't like it. Not one little bit.

He gave me a lecture about not poking my nose into police business, and I promised faithfully I wouldn't. So by the time he got in his car and drove off, I think we were friends once more. Just.

Perhaps I should have told him that sometimes my nose seems to have a mind of its own . . .

Chapter Four

I had to run to catch up with the others. By the time I did, they were halfway down the hill on which Courtenay House stood. Most of it was a large ornamental garden, but one part was quite wild, with trees and bushes surrounding a rocky outcrop.

The campsite was in a field at the bottom, next to an orchard. There was a toilet and shower block, sixteen tents for us kids, and an individual tent for every teacher.

Our tents were in two equal groups of eight. The girls would be sleeping in those to the right of the toilet block, the boys in those to the left. Mr Pinkerton said each tent was supposed to have room for four occupants. Sure, I thought. So long as two of them cut their legs off first.

Even if they did, we still had a problem. There were thirty-two girls on this year's school journey, and thirty-three boys. So if you know your four times table, you'll realize that meant the girls fitted into eight tents exactly. But eight weren't enough to accommodate all the boys. There was one boy too many.

Trust them to be awkward, I thought.

'There's nothing for it,' said Mr Pinkerton. 'We'll just have to squeeze five boys into one tent. What about that bunch over there? They always seem very friendly with each other.'

Everyone turned to stare at The Feeble Five. But four-fifths of them didn't jump at the chance the headmaster was offering. In fact, Greenstreet's pals turned pale and started to back away from their leader. It was obvious they weren't very keen on

Greenstreet's pals turned pale.....

having him in their tent. And we all knew why.

It *had* been a long, hot morning. You could almost see the poisonous fumes seeping out of Greenstreet's soles.

A ripple of panic passed through the other boys. If his gang didn't want Greenstreet in their tent, he might be foisted on someone else. The girls had already sorted themselves out perfectly into groups of four. Now the boys simply left as wide a space as possible around Greenstreet.

I noticed something else, too. My deadliest enemy usually likes to keep his gang with him, so they're always ready to make trouble. But one glance at his ugly face told me he didn't want to share with *them*, either. He just stood there looking worried, that zip-up bag still clutched under his arm.

I was becoming more and more curious about what it contained.

'I don't think *that* would work,' said Mrs Patel firmly.

'Have you got a better idea, Mrs Patel?' said Mr Pinkerton.

I dropped my rucksack and sleeping bag and sat down. I knew what was coming next. Our teachers were about to get stuck into a row while we slowly boiled in the afternoon heat. That's how it went, too. I reckon we'd still be there now if it hadn't been for Mrs Sternwood.

'Oh, for heaven's sake!' she said at last. 'This isn't getting us anywhere. He can have *my* tent if it's any help . . .'

Within a few minutes it was

settled. Greenstreet got Mrs Sternwood's tent, while she doubled up with Mrs Patel.

We spent the next couple of hours unpacking and settling in. I was sharing with Donna, Jackie and Charlotte, who couldn't stop talking about food. I was ravenous myself, so I was glad we'd been told to bring a packed lunch.

Later, I went in search of Richard. I came across him near the toilet block, but he didn't see me even when I was practically in front of him. He was too busy looking back up the hill, one hand shielding his eyes from the sun. He made me think of a pirate scanning the horizon.

'Let me know when you sight land, Cap'n,' I said, and poked him in the ribs. 'Then we can both go and dig up the treasure.'

'Oh, it's you, Sam,' he said. 'I was just trying to figure out where the cave might be . . .'

Then he began telling me some legend he'd discovered from hundreds of years ago about the hill containing a hidden cave. No-one had ever been able to find the entrance.

'Er, very interesting, Richard,' I said, quickly cutting him off before he got into his stride. 'But I was wondering if I could pick your brains on another subject . . .'

Richard is the sort of friend every detective needs. He reads all the time, so he knows lots of stuff. Most of it is mega-boring, but sometimes it turns out to be very useful.

'Has it got something to do with the Smith and Wesson case?' he said eagerly. 'That sounds really exciting!'

'Of course not!' I said firmly. From the corner of my eye I'd seen Mrs Patel approaching. I smiled at her as she walked past. 'You know I'm working on something *completely different* now.'

Richard should have known, although he'd probably been deep in a book when everyone else on the camp-site heard Mr Pinkerton ticking me off for upsetting Sir Nicholas. The headmaster had given me until dinnertime tonight to come up with another theme for my school journey project.

I wasn't going to drop the Smith and Wesson case, though. I'd just have to fool Mr Pinkerton by working on it undercover. I did have a substitute theme in mind – 'The Courtenay Family, Past and Present'. Old Pinkerton would like that. I thought it best not to tell him my *real* reason for choosing it.

I suspected the family and the case were linked.

When I'd mentioned the bandits, Sir Nicholas had got too angry, too fast. They'd definitely been identified as the two men seen near Courtenay House. So why deny it? Alarm bells had rung in my mind. When an adult behaves like that, there's usually only one reason. He's got something to hide.

'Actually, Richard,' I whispered when Mrs Patel had gone, 'I *am* still working on the Smith and Wesson disappearance. But you've got to keep that to yourself, OK?'

'Sure, Sam,' Richard whispered back, a gleam in his eyes now. 'You can trust me. But how can *I* help?'

'I've got a hunch the Courtenay family might be involved,' I said. 'Although I'm not absolutely sure yet. So I want you to tell me *everything* you know about them.'

I realized I should have chosen my words more carefully when Richard started talking about some guy called Sir Lancelot Courtenay. I ruled him out of the investigation immediately. There wouldn't have been much point in checking him out. He'd been a stiff for over five hundred years.

Richard then went on to give me a long, dull history lecture. It turned out he knew a great deal about the Courtenay family's distant past, and nothing about its present. By the time I'd got him to stop, I felt as if I were being smothered in ancient dust and cobwebs.

'I'm sorry, Richard,' I said, 'but

none of that is any use to me at all. What I need is the lowdown on Sir Nicholas High-and-Mighty himself, not his dead ancestors.'

'You could try the public library,' said Richard. He was looking a little crestfallen. 'I can think of a couple of reference books which would have some information on him. And there's bound to be something in back issues of the local paper. They keep those there, too, on computer.'

'That's my boy,' I said, and smiled. Richard smiled back.

We'd been given a timetable for the week already. It was packed with activities, but we *were* allowed some 'free' time, during which we were supposed to work on our projects. Richard and I agreed we'd go to the library in Stembridge the next day.

I said goodbye and went back to my tent. I wanted to read some of the notes about the Smith and Wesson case I'd brought with me. It was important I had the details at my fingertips before I started my

I pulled an exercise book out of my rucksack.

investigation. Luckily, my tent-mates were out somewhere, so I wouldn't be disturbed for a while.

I pulled an exercise book out of my rucksack, sat down, and began to read.

Smith and Wesson had become notorious last year with a series of bank robberies. They had done one a month, always on the seventh. The banks they hit also featured the number seven – the address of one was 77 High Street, for example, and another only had seven people working there.

One newspaper had called them 'The Lucky Number Bandits', and the name had stuck. Then the robbers had started leaving notes signed 'Smith and Wesson', thanking the banks and the police for making their work so easy. Unlike most villains, they obviously loved publicity.

They had fooled the boys in blue every time, too. They did a third job, a fourth, and a fifth, and the cops never even came close. On the sixth heist, a security camera got some film of them. It showed two men, but only one clearly, and he was wearing a mask which covered everything but his ears.

After that they wrote to the newspapers and really made fun of the old Bill. They even said 'The police can't hold a candle to us!' I remember thinking they might have gone just a little too far . . . and I was right.

The seventh target had been a bank in Garton, seven miles from their last job, and the biggest they'd tackled. But this time the police had done their homework, and the bank was staked out. When Smith and Wesson emerged with their loot, the place was entirely surrounded.

Even so, they *still* managed to get away. There was a wild car chase and the police lost them, although they were spotted on the Stembridge road, and by a vicar near Courtenay House. That had been five months ago, and nothing more had been heard of The Lucky Number Bandits. They had completely disappeared.

There had been no more raids, no notes, no letters to the newspapers . . . and no leads. Darkness had settled over the case like night falling, I thought as I closed the exercise book.

But now perhaps I'd seen a chink of light.

Chapter Five

At seven o'clock that evening we went up to the cafeteria in the big house for dinner. I told Mr Pinkerton the new theme for my project, and he positively beamed at me.

'That's *much* better, Sarah,' he said. 'Well done. I knew you could be a good girl if only you tried.'

I *hate* it when adults talk to me like that. I nearly kicked him in the knee, but I controlled myself. For the time being, I'd decided to keep a low profile as far as my teachers were concerned. I'd get on a lot faster with this case if I didn't have to deal with a load of stupid adults all the time.

That didn't necessarily apply to the Courtenays. I now realized I should have tried to make friends. I might be stuck if I couldn't get at least *some* information from them. But I wasn't worried. Even though we'd got off to a bad start, I can be a killer when it comes to turning on the charm.

They weren't in the cafeteria, worse luck. Lord and Lady Muck were being served by their butler elsewhere, according to Mr Pinkerton. He didn't say so, but he implied that the cafeteria was only good enough for the likes of common, vulgar people such as me and the other kids. He forgot *he* was with us too.

The food was good, though, and I was enjoying it so much I nearly missed what Mrs Sternwood said to him. She had been walking round the tables checking on everybody.

'I've done another count, Mr Pinkerton, and it's the same, I'm afraid. One of the boys is definitely missing.'

Mr Pinkerton sighed, did his eye-rolling, give-me-strength look, and put down his knife and fork.

'This really isn't good enough,' he said, crossly. 'I distinctly recall saying a staff member should check the campsite so no-one would get left behind.'

'Actually,' said Mrs Sternwood with a smile, 'you said *you* would do the checking.'

'Did I?' said Mr Pinkerton, his cheeks and bald scalp slowly turning red. He started to bluster. 'Well, of course, when I said *I* would do it, what I *meant* was . . .'

We never did find out what he meant.

A piercing scream suddenly split the warm evening air outside. When it stopped, the cafeteria was hushed for an instant, although I thought I could hear the faint sound of hairs standing up on the backs of everyone's necks.

Then there was pandemonium.

Mrs Sternwood dashed out, and was followed by Mrs Patel, Mr

Pinkerton, and the other teachers. Behind them swarmed a mob of Chandler Street kids hoping to see some blood.

I concentrated on my dinner while the crowd fought to get through the door. I already knew what had happened.

The scream had probably come from the person stupid enough to try searching my things. I'd left a surprise hidden under the flap of my rucksack. It was designed to keep my notes on the Smith and Wesson case safe from any intruder. I had a name for the most likely suspect, too.

Greenstreet, of course.

The door banged open, and everyone tumbled back in again. Mrs Sternwood had her arm round Greenstreet's shoulders. He was snivelling and holding his right hand. I could see the fingertips throbbing like those of a cartoon character after a close encounter with a mousetrap.

And that's exactly what he'd had.

Not so long ago at home we'd been

bothered by mice in the kitchen. Mum
had insisted we put down some traps,
although we'd never caught anything.
Your average mouse has obviously got
more brains than Greenstreet. More
personality, too.

I'd hung on to one of the traps,
though. I'd had a feeling it might come
in useful.

'If this is somebody's idea of a joke,'
Mr Pinkerton said, holding the mousetrap up for everyone to see, 'I don't
think it's very funny. I want to know

which of you little savages put it in Stuart's bag . . .'

How cunning, I thought. Greenstreet must have had time to get back to his tent. That way he'd avoided any awkward questions about what he'd been doing in mine. He'd also thought of a good explanation for the mousetrap. We all knew it was a trick almost every kid in the school would have loved to play on him.

'I'm waiting,' Mr Pinkerton said, impatiently tapping his foot. I noticed he'd spilt gravy down the front of his shell suit. 'Someone had better own up, or else . . .'

Nobody stepped forward. Greenstreet and I were the only people who knew the truth, anyway. His eyes sought me out across the cafeteria. Even though I'd won this particular battle, I could tell he wanted to keep the war going.

Then I realized *I* didn't. I sighed. Life's too short to spend half of it worrying about what a twerp like Greenstreet is doing, I thought.

Suddenly I was determined to come up with something that would get him off my back.

Permanently.

No-one took the rap for the mousetrap caper, so you won't be very surprised to hear we *all* had an early night. We slid into our sleeping bags, our ears ringing from Mr Pinkerton's dire warnings about what he'd do if we didn't shape up.

I'd checked my rucksack, and nothing was missing. The trap had worked. I didn't know what Greenstreet had been after, but I was pretty sure he'd think twice before trying again soon. So even though Donna, Jackie and Charlotte snored like pigs with bad colds, I slept very soundly.

A bit too soundly, in fact. I woke late, and dashed off to the girls' part of the shower block. It was chaos in there, of course, with everyone elbowing each other out of the way to get at the sinks, and yelling at the tops of their voices. The boys' side sounded even worse.

Then Mrs Sternwood came in and said we'd better hurry, or we'd miss breakfast. That made us move quickly, and soon we were in the cafeteria tucking in. It was great, and once we'd finished, we were ready to set off for the first activity on our timetables – Sir Nicholas's guided tour of Courtenay House.

Trips round old mansions have never really been my cup of tea. The only history I'm usually interested in is the kind you find in a villain's police file. But as you can imagine, I felt differently about this particular educational visit.

Sir Nicholas was waiting for us in the entrance hall. It had doors everywhere you looked, and an enormous sweeping staircase with bannisters that would have made a great slide. I didn't suggest we try it out, though. Somehow I don't think Sir Nicholas would have approved.

I was standing right in front of him. I gave him a big smile, but he didn't respond. He stared down his long, thin nose at me as if I was something that had crawled out from beneath a rock. Up close I thought his ears looked even bigger.

'Is everybody here?' he said at last. Mr Pinkerton nodded. 'Good. One usually begins the tour on the ground floor . . .'

We trailed through room, after room, after room, Sir Nicholas droning on about the history of each one. Richard wrote down everything he said in a small notebook.

I had a notebook too, but that was only for show. I was looking for clues that might explain what Sir Nicholas had to hide. But he gave nothing away, and I didn't see anything suspicious. After a while I began to wish Courtenay House was smaller. A lot smaller.

We came at last to a corridor Sir Nicholas called The Long Gallery. Both walls were covered with large paintings of people. I noticed most of them had big ears.

'These, of course, are one's ancestors,' said Sir Nicholas, stopping before the first picture. 'For example, this fierce-looking chap with the sword is . . .'

'It's Sir Lancelot Courtenay,' interrupted Richard. Oh no, not Sir Lancelot again, I thought. 'Born 1431, died 1489.'

'I say,' said Sir Nicholas, looking pleased. 'How jolly clever of you. Do you know any of the others?'

'Yes,' said Richard. 'The next one is Sir Lancelot's son . . .'

Richard, it turned out, knew who they all were. He almost took over the tour, and by the time we'd reached the last two pictures, which were of Sir Nicholas's father, and a young Sir Nicholas himself, I could see his lordship was very impressed.

'Bravo!' he said.

Richard smiled shyly, and Mr Pinkerton looked as happy as he had done the day he got his new car.

'Excuse me,' I said. 'But isn't someone missing?'

Richard, it turned out, knew who they all were.

I pointed at the wall next to the painting of Sir Nicholas. There was a faint outline, a square of unfaded wallpaper the same size as each of the other pictures.

Everything went very quiet for a second. Sir Nicholas turned his gaze on me. He looked as if there were a very nasty smell under his nose. Then he spun round and strode towards the end staircase. Mr Pinkerton gave me a look so full of daggers I almost ducked. Mrs Sternwood just tutted and shook her head.

'I was only asking,' I said, but no-one listened.

My schoolmates brushed past me as they followed Sir Nicholas. I slowly edged my way to the wall. I'd seen something interesting off to one side – another, smaller staircase that led upwards. A short, thick rope with golden tassels was looped across. A sign saying 'Private' hung from it.

Time to do a little exploring on my own, I thought as I stepped over the rope . . .

Chapter Six

I crept up the stairs and paused at the top. I'd come to another corridor, but this one was very different.

It wasn't so long, for a start. There were three doors with tables beside them, on each of which was a pot plant. Everything seemed much . . . well, *cosier* was the only word that came to mind. Then it dawned on me. This was where Sir Nicholas and Lady Jennifer must actually live.

There was no-one in sight, so I tiptoed over to the nearest door. It was slightly ajar, and through the crack I saw Lady Jennifer sitting in an armchair, a sad expression on her face. She was leafing through something

67

that looked like a photograph album, the sort you keep old family snaps in.

I moved silently to the next door, which was shut. I quietly opened it, peeked round, and found a large, luxurious bedroom. The third door was directly opposite, next to a second small staircase which seemed to lead down to the rear of the house. I eased over and tried the handle. The door was locked.

There was no key, either. I started to wonder where it might be hidden, but I soon stopped. Without warning, a strong hand landed on my shoulder. If my mouth hadn't been shut tight my heart would have leaped out of it.

'Can I help you, Miss?' somebody said.

I looked round . . . and breathed a sigh of relief. It was only Walters, the butler. He released his grip. I realized he must have come up the other small staircase without my hearing.

'Maybe you can,' I said, thinking quickly. 'I, er . . . got separated from the rest of my class.'

'You certainly won't find your party
behind that door, Miss,' said Walters.
'Now, if you would be so kind as to
follow me . . .'

He walked along the corridor to the
staircase I'd come up originally. I
hadn't taken much notice of him
before, but now I noticed he was tall
and broad-shouldered. He seemed
more like a body-builder than a butler.
But then perhaps butlers need to be

strong. We've never had one at home, so I wouldn't know.

'Is anything wrong, Walters?' said Lady Jennifer. She must have heard our voices and come out to see what was going on.

'No, Ma'am,' said Walters, 'nothing at all. The young lady was lost, and I am simply taking her back to the others.'

'These are our private apartments,' said Lady Jennifer suspiciously, turning to me. 'There's a sign.'

'I'm afraid I didn't see it,' I said. Time to switch on the Marlowe charm, I thought, and smiled. 'I'm *awfully* sorry, and I promise it won't happen again. But I was wondering . . .'

'Well, make sure it doesn't,' said Lady Jennifer, and closed the door in my face. So much for my devastating charm.

'This way, Miss,' said Walters, and walked off. I had to hurry. It was hard keeping pace with his long stride.

'What *is* in that room anyway?' I asked when I caught up with him.

'Why is it locked? Is something valuable stored in there?'

'I'm afraid only Sir Nicholas or Lady Jennifer could answer your questions, Miss,' he said as we went down the stairs. 'I've only been with them a few months, and I've still got an awful lot to find out about the house and the family.'

You and me both, pal, I thought.

I had been going to ask Lady Jennifer if I could come and talk to her about my school project. But it was clear I wouldn't have got very far even if she'd let me finish what I was saying. It was beginning to look as if all I'd ever get from the Courtenays was a hard time.

But I had seen some interesting things. Or rather, I *hadn't* seen them. A missing picture, whatever was in that locked room . . . I was sure now this family had something to hide.

My job was simple. I just had to uncover it.

The others were heading for the

garden when Walters found them. He didn't say anything, and none of the teachers seemed to have noticed my absence. Sir Nicholas was still talking, and their attention was focused on him. I slipped into the crowd, and when I looked round, Walters had vanished.

Once the guided tour was over, we went for lunch in the cafeteria. It was just as good as dinner and breakfast had been. The only problem was the vile stench coming from Greenstreet's trainers.

'What are we supposed to be doing this afternoon, Richard?' I said, holding my nose. I'd forgotten to bring my timetable.

'We're going to the church down the road, I think,' he said, looking at his. A big smile lit his face. 'Mrs Sternwood reckons we might even be able to do some brass rubbing.'

'Wow, Richard,' I said. 'I can't stand the excitement.'

As you might have guessed, that's not what I really thought. To tell the truth, it sounded like a trip straight to Boredom City, and I'd spent more than enough time there for one day. It was a nuisance, too. I was as certain as I could be that it wouldn't get me any further with my case.

But I was wrong.

We walked in a long crocodile to the church, led by Mr Pinkerton in his dazzling shell suit. It was another hot day, and we stood waiting in the graveyard while the headmaster went to find the vicar. At last they came out together, and Mr Pinkerton told us to gather round.

The vicar was a short, plump man with sandy hair. Unlike Mr Pinkerton, who was sweating a lot, the vicar didn't seem to be affected by the heat at all, even though he was wearing a long, black cassock and a tight dog collar.

'Good afternoon, children,' he said in a high, sing-song voice. 'Welcome to the Church of St Olaf and The Holy Trinity. My name is Reverend Holmes . . .'

73

Something peculiar happened to the vicar's face as he was talking. His eyes crinkled up, his mouth went into a thin, straight line, and his cheeks bulged. It reminded me of a balloon being squeezed in the middle. Reverend Holmes was smiling. I just hoped he didn't go pop.

Then something did exactly that, but only in my brain, thank goodness. Reverend Holmes had a very familiar name, and being a super-sleuth, I instantly called to mind where I'd come across it before. It had been in most of the newspapers when Smith and Wesson had disappeared.

He was the vicar who had spotted them near Courtenay House!

Suddenly I was desperate to talk to him. He had actually *seen* The Lucky Number Bandits, even if it had only been briefly! But I had to wait while we got another guided tour, this time round the church and the graveyard, which seemed to contain all Sir Nicholas's ancestors.

'Thank you *so* much, Reverend

Sloane,' said Mr Pinkerton at last. His bald pate gleamed with sweat. 'I'm sure the children will agree with me when I say everything you've told us was *very* interesting. Now, I think the plan was to split up into smaller groups, wasn't it, Mrs Stevens?'

This was my chance. The teachers were taking groups off for various

This was my chance...

activities, such as the brass rubbing Richard was so keen on. I was supposed to be with the group detailed to draw pictures of the stained-glass windows. But I had other plans. I hid behind a large tomb till everyone had dispersed.

'Excuse me, Reverend Holmes,' I said, when the coast was clear. He was picking up an empty crisp packet from the path. 'I wonder if you could possibly help me with my school project? I've got a few questions . . .'

'Of course, my dear,' he said. 'Fire away.'

I began with some enquiries about the link between St Olaf's and the Courtenays. Reverend Holmes said it had been the family church for hundreds of years, which was something I'd already worked out for myself. Most of the ancestors whose pictures Sir Nicholas had shown us were buried there.

Then I hit the vicar with the big one.

'Ah, Reverend,' I said, as cool as an

ice cube. I had to be very careful. If I handled this wrong, I might not get anywhere. Sometimes adults can be funny about what they'll tell kids. 'I've just remembered. Didn't I read that you were an important witness in a police case?'

'I'd hardly say I was *important*,' he said. 'I merely did what any good citizen would have done in the circumstances . . .'

I relaxed. By slipping the subject in casually, I hadn't made him suspicious. In fact, he seemed to enjoy talking about it. Pretty soon the Reverend was giving me the whole story.

On that evening five months ago, Reverend Holmes had set off by bike to see one of his parishioners, an old lady who had recently been ill. Her cottage was on the main road, a mile or so beyond Courtenay House. As he'd gone past the gate, he'd noticed a car parked beside the tree, with two men inside it.

He hadn't been able to see them

clearly, but he was fairly certain they had been arguing.

He had thought no more of it until he'd watched the TV news later, and recognized a description of Smith and Wesson's getaway car. He rang the police immediately, but when they investigated, the car had gone. It was discovered abandoned in the woods a couple of days later.

'For a week, Stembridge was *full* of police,' said Reverend Holmes, 'and they all seemed terribly busy. That's why I didn't bother them with what I found the next morning.'

'What was that, Reverend?' I asked, intrigued.

'Oh, just some blood on a head-stone,' he said, giving me another of his squashed-balloon smiles. 'But there were only two or three drops . . .'

Chapter Seven

I stood stunned for a second, unable to quite believe what I'd heard. So I asked him to say it again.

'I found two or three drops of blood on a headstone,' he said. He had stopped smiling, and seemed worried. 'You don't think I should have informed the police, do you?'

'That depends on whose blood it was, Reverend,' I said. 'Did you have any idea where it came from?'

'Not at first,' said the vicar, 'although it did give me a bit of a turn, I don't mind telling you, especially after the excitement of the night before. Then I realized I was being a silly Billy, and assumed a fox had caught a rabbit in the graveyard. I often come across the odd paw or piece of fur.'

'I can imagine,' I said, my mind full of the kind of gory pictures you get in wildlife programmes on TV. 'Could you show me which headstone it was?'

'Why yes,' said the reverend. 'It was this one here. You're standing right next to it.'

I should have guessed it would be Sir Lancelot's. He might have been dead for five hundred years, but he still managed to pop up everywhere I went. He was beginning to get on my nerves.

I bent down to examine the old stone. It was a metre high, and leant to one side. Reverend Holmes couldn't remember exactly where he'd seen the drops. So I ran my fingers over the rough surface, and examined several faint stains. But there was nothing much to see.

Maybe this *was* a vital clue, I thought. The reverend had seen the two men in the car *arguing*, hadn't he?

I should have guessed it would be Sir Lancelot.

Their argument could easily have led to a fight, and the fight might well have ended in blood. It was a neat theory . . . but if it was correct, it left me with a lot more questions than I'd started with.

What had Smith and Wesson been arguing about? Why had they come to the church, and what had happened there? To which one had the blood belonged? And most important, if one of them had been injured, how had he got away? Maybe he hadn't, I thought suddenly. This was a graveyard, after all . . .

But then that was a lot to base on two or three drops of blood. It could certainly have happened the way the reverend thought. It *was* the simpler, more logical answer. And I wasn't in the business of catching foxes for doing what came naturally. No, I was on the trail of some human scavengers.

Reverend Holmes was still looking concerned, though. I realized that if I let him know what I'd been thinking, he'd almost certainly want to tell the police. And I wasn't ready to let them muscle in on my case yet. I had no proof of anything, anyway. So I decided to calm him down.

'I think you were right not to bother the police, Reverend,' I said, giving him a reassuring smile. 'I'm sure it *was* a fox and a rabbit. Bad luck for the bunny, that's what I say.'

Reverend Holmes seemed satisfied with that. I wanted to ask him a few more questions, but I didn't get the chance.

'Ah, there you are, Samantha,' said Mrs Sternwood. She'd come up behind us, and sounded cross. 'I wondered where you'd got to. I do hope she hasn't been bothering you, Reverend.'

'Not at all,' said the vicar. 'Indeed, we've been having a most interesting conversation about . . .'

'About my school project, actually,' I said hurriedly. 'It's been very useful, but I think I'd better be running along now. Thanks, Reverend! Bye!'

'Oh, goodbye, dear,' said the vicar.

He was looking a little confused. 'I'm glad I could be of some help . . .'

He might have been, I thought, as I ran off. And then again, he might not. Either way, I was glad I'd come to the church and met Reverend Holmes. The stuff about Smith and Wesson arguing was *very* interesting. And as for the blood . . . It was definitely something to bear in mind.

For the first time since we'd arrived, I felt I was actually beginning to get somewhere with this case.

But there was still an awful long way to go.

'How much further is it, Sir?' whined Greenstreet.

He'd done nothing but moan all morning, except when he'd been calling me names or trying to push me into a stream. He hadn't succeeded, and in general I'd managed to keep out of his way. I wanted our country walk to be over as much as he did. But not for the same reasons. Mostly I was just bored with *him*.

Greenstreet hates any form of physical exercise. I don't mind it, although I could definitely have done without today's two-hour hike in the heat. It was on the timetable though, so there was no getting out of it. At least that's what Mr Pinkerton had said. By now he probably wished he hadn't.

'Nearly there, Stuart,' he gasped, sweat dripping off his bushy eyebrows as he plodded along. His shell suit was starting to look crumpled. 'We just have to . . . keep . . . going . . .'

We finally made it to the campsite entrance at the bottom of the hill. We hadn't used it before. There was no car-park, which was why the coach driver had dropped us off at the front gate. Mr Pinkerton had to keep his car in a small area off the gravel drive, near a side exit from Courtenay House.

Next came lunch, and then we were on free time. Most of my classmates were too exhausted to do anything but collapse in their tents. But I felt OK.

I collected my Smith and Wesson notes, and rounded up Richard. He was tired, but willing.

We had a date with some books and a computer.

We caught the bus into town. The library was easy to find. It was an old building with double doors just behind the Post Office. A nice lady with short blonde hair stood behind a long desk inside. She smiled as we came in.

'Can I help you?' she said.

We asked her where the reference section was, and she told us. Now it was up to Richard.

I wasn't worried, though. He was obviously pretty comfortable in a library. He went straight over to the shelves and pulled out a couple of big, fat books. He brought them over and dumped them on the table in front of me.

'This one is *Who's Who*,' he whispered. 'It lists the important people in the country, and tells you something about them. The other one is smaller, but it concentrates on people with titles, like Lord and Lady Courtenay.'

'Well, what are we waiting for?' I said. 'Let's get to it.'

We sat down and opened one book each. I turned to 'C' for Courtenay in *Who's Who*, and spent the next ten minutes reading about Sir Nicholas. I found out lots of things, like when he'd been born, where he'd gone to school, and what his hobbies were. There was nothing about crime being one of them.

The other book covered much the same ground, although it did have a section about the history of the family, and how they'd got their title. Richard asked me if I wanted to read it myself. But I said I'd give it a miss. I had no desire to bump into Sir Lancelot again, even if it was only in print.

'Are you *sure*, Sam?' said Richard. He seemed amazed I wasn't interested. 'You never know, there might be a clue . . .'

'I doubt it, Richard,' I said. 'Now, didn't you mention something about the local newspaper being stored on computer? I think I'm more likely to get a lead out of *that*.'

I didn't have to ask him twice. If there's one thing Richard loves even more than books, it's playing with computers. He led me over to a keyboard and screen in the corner of the reference section. His fingers flew over the keys, and soon we were browsing through page after page of The *Stembridge Gazette*.

We went backwards, stopping briefly every time we saw a piece about the Courtenays. There were quite a few stories, too, although they usually only featured Lady Jennifer opening a new playgroup, or Sir Nicholas visiting an old people's home. Very noble, I'm sure . . . but very boring, too.

We carried on, although I was beginning to think it might be a waste of time. Then something caught my eye.

'Hold it, Richard,' I said. 'I want to read this properly.'

Richard kept the page on the screen. It was an interview with Sir Nicholas, in which he explained why he'd opened Courtenay House to the public. The reason had been simple. A stately home is very expensive to run, and the family just couldn't afford it any more. They needed the cash tourists brought in.

Ah ha, I thought. *Very* interesting.

Another story in the same issue was even more enlightening, though. The paper had done a whole spread on The Lucky Number Bandits after their disappearance. At first I thought it told me nothing I didn't know already, and I nearly told Richard to move on. Then I saw the map.

It showed the places where Smith and Wesson had done their raids. I suddenly realized they formed a perfect circle round Stembridge. There it was, slap bang in the middle, with Courtenay House very close.

Other detectives would have stopped there, I suppose, happy with the afternoon's work. It *was* plenty to be going on with. But I had a feeling something else was waiting for me inside the computer, a clue that might lead me straight to the heart of this strange mystery. I was right, too.

'Keep going, Richard,' I said.

The pages flowed past my eyes. The screen's green, flickering glow was starting to make them itchy. But they were still sharp enough to spot the most important fact of all. The name Edward Courtenay kept cropping up. Lord and Lady Jennifer apparently had a grown-up son.

And *he* had gone missing too.

Chapter Eight

I soon discovered Edward Courtenay had been quite a character. As far as I could tell, he had tried every dangerous sport known to the human race, and a couple he seemed to have invented himself. This was a guy who needed excitement like other people needed fresh air. He got a lot of both.

Up until about a year and a half ago, *The Stembridge Gazette* had been full of his exploits. There were stories about him jumping out of planes and climbing mountains. He'd crossed the Sahara desert on a camel, and the Arctic in a sledge. Then he'd gone up the Amazon in a canoe.

And he hadn't come back.

It was all there in black and green. How he'd failed to return when he was due, how a search party was sent and found nothing, how Lord and Lady Courtenay had been deeply concerned. I could understand that. They might be aristocrats, but they probably had feelings just like the rest of us.

Since then there had been no news. Edward Courtenay had vanished from the face of the Earth. Unless . . .

Unless, I thought, it had been a set-up.

There was another way of looking at the facts I'd collected. What if the Courtenays hadn't solved their money problems? Their son might have wanted to help out his parents by robbing a few banks. He obviously liked life in the fast lane, and crime can be *very* exciting – so long as you don't get caught.

A good way of preventing that is to make everyone think you don't exist any more. Perhaps he had staged his disappearance, then slipped back into the country in disguise. Being the son of a Lord and Lady was a pretty good cover for starters. Vanishing would make it almost perfect.

You could hardly be suspected of a series of crimes here if everyone thought you'd died in South America.

'Are you OK, Sam?' said Richard, breaking my train of thought. 'You've been sitting there staring for ages.'

'What? Oh, I'm fine, Richard,' I said, rubbing my eyes. 'I was just doing some thinking, that's all.'

Richard asked if I'd seen enough, and I said I had. He went to put the two books back on the shelves. I knew he wanted to look up some information for his project, so I told him I'd wait outside. I walked out of the library and found a bench nearby where I could sit in the sunshine.

A pigeon pecked at something on the pavement while I let things come together in my mind. Everything pointed to Courtenay House as a base for The Lucky Number Bandits, although I couldn't prove it yet. But even if I was right about Edward

Courtenay, I still had some un-answered questions.

I had no idea who his partner was, for a start. Smith and Wesson must have been assumed names, but I didn't think they had been a father and son double act. Sir Nicholas was too old to go jumping over bank counters with a gun. That wasn't my only reason for feeling he didn't fit the part, though.

I kept thinking about a painting, the one that should have been in The Long Gallery, and wasn't.

I was convinced it could only be a picture of Edward. The others went in order of descent, and he was the last of the Courtenays. But why had it been taken down? You'd have thought Sir Nicholas and Lady Jennifer would want it there to remind them of their missing son. They obviously didn't.

What if they'd found out about their son becoming a bank robber, and hadn't approved?

Most parents would have been upset by something like that. They

might have said they didn't want anything more to do with him, which
would explain the missing picture.
They'd definitely try to keep their
son's new sport quiet, and that could
explain the way Sir Nicholas had
reacted to me.

The last thing he'd want was
someone snooping around and coming
up with a black sheep in the family.

He'd be even more nervous because
of all the publicity. Then I realized
that fitted the pattern, too. The
Edward Courtenay I'd read about in
The Stembridge Gazette wouldn't have
been able to resist showing off in the
newspapers. I'd bet my bottom dollar
he even enjoyed making things more
risky for himself that way.

Suddenly the sun went behind a
small cloud, and the pigeon flew off.
Get a grip on yourself, Marlowe, I
thought. This was starting to sound
like some kind of crazy fantasy. I only
needed to be wrong about a tiny bit of
it for the whole thing to collapse like
a house of cards.

And I still didn't know what had happened to Smith and Wesson, or whether the blood in the churchyard had belonged to one of them. There was probably a much simpler explanation.

But somehow I didn't think so.

'Are you ready, Sam?' asked Richard. I didn't reply. 'Sam? What are you staring at now?'

'Isn't that Walters, the butler?' I said. 'I wonder what *he* was doing in there?'

I'd seen him come out of the library behind Richard. He had glanced in my direction, then looked away. I wasn't sure he'd recognized me. Now he was walking briskly down the street.

'Returning his books, I should think,' said Richard. 'That's what people usually do when they go to the library, isn't it?'

'You're probably right,' I said.

I tried to put Walters out of my mind. But the sight of him had made me feel uneasy. I thought of the nasty

There was probably a much simpler explanation....

shock he'd given me outside that locked room in Courtenay House.

Then it happened again.

'Hello, hello, hello,' said a slow voice as a hand squeezed my shoulder. 'Fancy meeting *you* here.'

I turned round and found myself looking up at a face with twinkly blue eyes and a big smile. It was Sergeant Cuff.

'Phew!' I said. 'Promise me you won't ever do that again. I nearly had a heart attack.'

'You must have a guilty conscience then,' he said. 'What have you been up to? Something I should arrest you for?'

'Not yet, Sarge,' I said. 'Actually, we've just been doing some research in the library.'

'I'm impressed,' said the sergeant. 'Sounds like thirsty work, though. How about a cold drink? My treat.'

There was a small kiosk on the corner. Sergeant Cuff bought Richard and me a can of Coke each. We said thanks. The sun had come out again, and it was very warm.

'So, what were you two looking up in the library?' said Sergeant Cuff. 'I hope it wasn't anything to do with that case we discussed when you arrived, Samantha . . .'

'Of course not,' I said before Richard could open his mouth and put his foot in it. Sergeant Cuff was giving me a very piercing stare, the sort that makes most people own up on the spot to any number of crimes. But not Sam Marlowe. 'I'm working on a new project now, the history of the Courtenay family . . .'

The sergeant seemed pleased. I asked him what he knew about the disappearance of Edward Courtenay, but he couldn't tell me much. As far as he was concerned, it had simply been a tragic episode which everyone in Stembridge regretted.

'Anyway Samantha, I'm glad to see you're managing to keep out of trouble,' he said. 'I don't think I could cope with any more problems at the moment.'

'That sounds interesting, Sarge,' I

said. 'Tell me more. Perhaps you need the assistance of an ace detective.'

'Nice of you to offer, Sam,' laughed Sergeant Cuff, 'but I don't think you can help. It's something that's had me and my men scratching our heads for the last few months, and we're still stumped.'

It seemed there had been a series of strange break-ins throughout the Stembridge area. They were peculiar mainly because nothing of any real value was ever stolen. It was usually only small amounts of food, or the odd bottle of milk. It happened regularly, but so far no clues had been found.

'Ah well, it's back to work for me, I suppose,' said Sergeant Cuff at last. 'I won't catch any villains if I sit round chatting to you all day. Nice to see you, Sam, and to meet your friend. But remember — just keep that nose of yours clean. I wouldn't want you to end up as one of my customers!'

'Don't worry, Sarge,' I said. 'You and I will always be on the same side.'

'That's a relief,' he said. 'At least, I *think* it is . . .'

If anyone else had come up with a smart remark like that, I would never have forgiven them. But I just laughed. Sergeant Cuff was OK, and I didn't mind a joke from him.

Besides, I had a feeling he'd be singing a different tune pretty soon. I knew I was on the point of cracking this case. I was sure I had most of the facts. I just needed to arrange them in the right order. Oh yes, and maybe find a little proof. But that was no problem. I had a good idea where it might be waiting for me.

We said goodbye and went our separate ways, Sergeant Cuff to the police station, Richard and I to the bus that would take us back to the campsite. Richard asked if our trip to the library had helped. I said it had, but I didn't tell him how.

'What's your next step then, Sam?' he asked, eagerly.

'I'm not sure, Richard,' I said. 'I'll have to wait and see.'

I don't like lying to Richard, but I didn't want to get him into trouble. I *did* have a plan, and if it went wrong, I wanted to make sure I'd be the only one who'd take the fall.

I was going to pay a visit to a certain locked room.

But this time no-one would stop me finding the key and getting inside . . .

Chapter Nine

I glided silently through the dark garden towards Courtenay House. The midnight sky was moonless, so I was glad Mum had persuaded me to bring a torch from home. Behind me lay the campsite. I'd waited until the others in my tent had started snoring, then I'd slipped out.

At dinner earlier that evening, I'd left a window in the cafeteria unlocked. I hoped I'd be able to open it from the outside. I held my breath as I slipped my fingers under the edge and pulled, half expecting an alarm to go off. But nothing happened, and I quickly climbed through.

My torch beam made spooky

shadows as I moved through the rooms. Soon I was stepping over that rope again, and climbing the small staircase. I peeked round at the top, but the corridor was deserted, and the three doors shut. I tiptoed to the one I wanted and tried the handle. It was still locked.

No problem. I had a good idea where the key might be. I turned to the table nearby and lifted up the pot plant. Hey presto – the key was lying underneath. I unlocked the door and went in. I shone my torch on the walls, and the first thing I noticed was a large picture. It was the missing painting.

So this was Edward Courtenay. He had his mother's eyes, but otherwise he looked just like his dad. He certainly had the family ears, and seeing them made me think of another picture, one taken during a bank raid. I imagined a mask over the face in the painting, and the two images merged in my mind.

This must have been Edward's

bedroom, I thought. There were some posters of racing cars and aeroplanes, a Persian rug, and a bed with a battered teddy bear on the pillow. And on top of a chest of drawers there was some sort of antique candle holder, complete with seven big candles.

Suddenly I heard footsteps outside. I desperately looked round, but there was no hiding place. I was caught.

'And what have you got to say for yourself, young lady?' said Sir Nicholas as he marched in and switched on the light. He was wearing a dressing gown, and looked furious.

Lady Jennifer was peering at me from behind her husband. She was in her dressing gown too, and her hair was full of curlers.

'Not much,' I said. 'Only that I'd like to talk to you about your son. The one who's a bank robber . . .'

'That's absolute nonsense . . .' spluttered Sir Nicholas.

'Oh, *do* be quiet Nicholas,' sighed Lady Jennifer. 'I can't stand the worry any more.'

I desperately looked around,
but there was no hiding place,
I was caught.

Sir Nicholas then gave me a real surprise. He sat down on his son's bed, his lips trembling . . . and burst into tears.

'There, there, dear,' said Lady Jennifer. She sat down too, and put her arm round his shoulders. 'Don't blame yourself.'

'Er . . . excuse me for interrupting,' I said. 'But would one of you like to tell me what's going on?'

That was all it took. Lady Jennifer had kept too much bottled up inside her for far too long. She just needed someone who would listen, and yours truly had volunteered for the job.

While she was speaking I heard a rustling noise coming from the garden. I went over to the window, and saw rain streaming down the panes. The dry spell had broken at last. There was a distant flash of lightning, and a low rumble of thunder.

It seemed I'd got almost everything right. The Courtenays *did* have money problems, and Edward *had* come up with a wild plan to help his parents by robbing banks. He *had* staged his disappearance in Brazil, then sneaked home. And Sir Nicholas and Lady Jennifer *had* disapproved.

'There was a terrible row,' said Lady Jennifer. 'Nicholas ordered Edward to give up his crazy scheme or get out and never come back. Edward said he'd be happy to go. I tried to stop him, and make them both see reason. It was no use, though. They're as stubborn and pig-headed as each other.'

I felt sorry for Lady Jennifer. She hadn't liked what her son had in mind, but she knew disowning him wouldn't be the answer. It was Sir Nicholas who'd taken down the picture, and Lady Jennifer who'd hung it in Edward's room. I'd bet she'd been looking at old photos of him when I'd seen her the day before.

'But what got him interested in crime?' I said.

'That's a question we've often asked ourselves,' said Lady Jennifer. 'And we think someone has led him astray. He once mentioned a man he'd met on an expedition, a chap who sounded rather, well . . . suspicious. He never told us his name, though.'

Edward had been very impressed by this shady character, a guy with a criminal record who'd done time in jail. Bingo, I thought. I was convinced this pal was the other robber.

I'd never met Edward, but I reckoned it wouldn't have been hard to tempt him into being a villain. For a start, he loved excitement, and he'd probably been running out of ideas for dangerous things to do. Even if he'd had second thoughts, I was sure the argument with his father had helped make up his mind.

My dad says the quickest way of getting *me* to do something is ordering me not to. I'd bet anything you like Edward was the same. I said as much to his parents.

'But he was such a *good* little boy,' said Lady Jennifer, picking up the teddy bear and hugging it. 'He loved his teddy, didn't he, dear? Do you remember how he couldn't stand being parted from him when he went away with the school that time?'

Now it was Lady Jennifer who began to cry, and Sir Nicholas who put his arm round *her* shoulders. A flash of lightning lit the window, and something sparked in my brain. Lady Jennifer's words had helped solve a mystery that had been bugging me since the first day of this trip.

But I had to forget about that for the time being.

The Courtenays hadn't seen or heard from Edward since the day of the row. At first they'd hoped he would come home, saying he'd been joking. But then the robberies had begun, and they soon realized he was involved. One thing gave him away. Seven had always been his lucky number.

'We were *very* worried, of course,' said Lady Jennifer, wiping her eyes with a small, lacy handkerchief, 'but we simply couldn't bring ourselves to tell the police. Edward *is* our son, after all. We thought that if we kept quiet, he might come to his senses before it was too late . . .'

'That's right,' said Sir Nicholas, 'but we've been frantic since the robberies stopped. If only we knew where he'd gone. You don't think he might have come to some harm, do you?'

The pair of them stared at me with their sad, wet eyes, and I thought about fights in graveyards and blood on headstones. I didn't mention either. I opened my mouth to say something reassuring, but then I closed it again. Two facts were pulling at each other in my mind like a pair of powerful magnets.

Seven was Edward's lucky number . . . And what was it Smith and Wesson had written in a letter to a newspaper? Something about the police not being able 'to hold a candle' to them . . . And hadn't I seen a candle holder when I'd come into Edward's bedroom? One with *seven* candles?

I strode across the room to look at that particular antique more closely.

I put my torch down on the chest of drawers, and examined each candle, starting from the left. They were smooth and waxy, as you'd expect. The last one, though – the seventh – was different. It wasn't waxy. It was plastic.

I lifted it out, and saw that it was hollow. Something was inside it, too, a rolled-up sheet of thick, dusty paper which I pulled out. I'd found another map, and this one showed there *was* a cave in the hill on which Courtenay House stood. Its entrance was concealed in the rocky outcrop I'd noticed.

But that wasn't all. The map revealed a secret passage that led from the cave right into the cellars of Courtenay House. Everything connected, it seemed, and not just on paper. For the map was dated 'This seventh day of July, AD 1477', and was signed in old-fashioned writing by . . . Sir Lancelot Courtenay.

I should have known he'd make one last appearance in this case. But this time I was pleased he had. There was some more writing on the map, and it told me Sir Lancelot had covered up the cave entrance and built the passage to provide a secret escape route if Courtenay House were ever attacked.

Over the years it had been forgotten. But Edward, it seemed, had been fascinated by his family's history. He had probably stumbled across the map during the long hours he'd spent poring over family books and documents. And it gave him the perfect spot to stash away his ill-gotten gains.

No wonder the robberies had formed a circle round Stembridge, I thought. After every raid the bandits had come to Courtenay House to hide their loot. Why keep the map, though? Edward hadn't needed it any more, and surely it would have been better not to take the risk that someone else would find it . . .

Then it dawned on me. The map had been a lucky charm for him, especially with those sevens in the date. He must have felt he'd never be caught so long as it was in that hollow candle. It wasn't any more, though, and I was hot on his trail. But there was no time to lose.

Sir Nicholas and Lady Jennifer, however, were confused. I'd been thinking aloud, but I'd lost them a long way back. My mind often works too fast for adults to keep up. I sighed, and quickly went over it all again.

'Brilliant,' said a voice behind me. 'Quite brilliant.'

I turned round to thank whoever had spoken, but my voice froze in my mouth. I couldn't believe what I was seeing. Then another piece of the puzzle clicked into place.

Walters was standing framed in the doorway. He was holding a gun, and it was aimed straight at . . . *me*!

Chapter Ten

'Good grief, Walters,' said Sir Nicholas. 'What in heaven's name are you doing? And where did you get that gun?'

'Shut up, you old fool,' snarled Walters, turning the pistol on the Courtenays. 'And put your hands up, all of you.'

We did as he said. Sir Nicholas and Lady Jennifer looked more confused than ever, but I saw everything as clear as day. And I'd been waiting my whole life to deliver the next line.

'Actually, Sir Nicholas, the butler did it,' I said. 'Along with your son, that is. Walters was Edward's partner in crime.'

'Ten out of ten,' said Walters, smiling. 'But then I knew you'd be the answer to my prayers. In fact, it's been a real education following you around, watching you work. Now, if you'll just hand over that map, I'll be on my way . . .

'Not so fast, buster,' I said, tucking it in a pocket. 'I want the whole story first. You owe me that, at least.'

'Fair enough,' said Walters. 'It can't matter much now . . .'

Walters talked about meeting Edward and persuading him that crime *could* pay. He'd come up with the Amazon plan, and he'd stayed behind to prepare for Edward's return. Then they'd started doing the robberies. Walters did the driving – and Edward said he had the perfect place to hide the loot.

There had been only one problem as far as Walters was concerned. Edward had refused to tell him exactly where the stash was. He had claimed it was safer that way. Walters had put up with it at first, but then Edward

116

had begun taking crazy risks. After the last job, Walters wanted out.

But Edward was enjoying himself too much. He was keen to carry on, and they'd argued when they'd reached Courtenay House about dividing the money. Then they'd split up as usual, Edward heading for the hideaway, Walters going off to ditch the car.

'I think *I* can fill in the rest,' I said. 'You met at the churchyard, where the argument turned into a fight. Edward was knocked down, and cracked his head against a tombstone. Then you fled, believing you'd killed him.'

'Oh no!' said Lady Jennifer, horrified. 'My poor boy!'

'Don't worry,' snarled Walters. 'There wasn't a body, was there? He must have come to after I'd left, and got away.'

'Where *is* he, then?' said Sir Nicholas anxiously.

'How should I know?' said Walters. 'I thought you might have been hiding him here, which is why I applied for the butler's job when I saw it advertised. I soon found out you weren't. So I concentrated on looking for the money instead . . . but I had no luck. Not until our little friend here turned up, anyway.'

So there it was. The whole scam zipped jerkily past inside my head like a movie on fast forward, one with an old plot. A family row, the lure of easy money, thieves falling out as they always do. It was almost time for the final credits. I had the names, though one of the stars was missing.

Then I remembered a conversation from earlier that day. Suddenly I *knew* where Edward Courtenay was, *and* what he'd been doing for the last five months. But the knowledge was useless while I was staring down the barrel of a gun.

A loud buzzing disturbed my thoughts, and I saw Walters start brushing impatiently at something near his face. A large fly was dive-bombing him. It reminded me a lot of the one I'd let out of my classroom window last week.

Hey, I thought. Maybe it *is* that fly, and he's come to return the favour. Old friend or not, he was doing all he could to distract Walters. I'd been offered a chance, and I took it with both hands. I bent down, grabbed the Persian rug . . . and pulled.

Walters flew over backwards. His gun went off and blew out the light, plunging the room into darkness. I dived for cover, and the next moment a flash of lightning showed me that Walters had gone. His gun lay on the rug by the open door.

'Call the police!' I said to Sir Nicholas and Lady Jennifer, who were peering out from underneath their son's bed. They both seemed OK. 'I'll try and stop him escaping!'

I picked up my torch and ran into the corridor, but there was no sign of the villain.

There was only one thing for it. I dashed to the main staircase,

straddled the bannisters, and let myself go. It was a fantastic ride. I felt like I was doing a hundred miles an hour . . . but about halfway down I started to wonder how I'd be able to stop. By then it was too late.

I zoomed off the end . . . and crashed into Mr Pinkerton, who had just come through the main doors into the entrance hall. As we hit the marble floor with a loud squelch, I glimpsed the rest of the Chandler Street party crowding in. The campsite must have been flooded out. They were all drenched.

'Oof!' said Mr Pinkerton. 'What the . . .'

'Can't stop to explain!' I shouted as I climbed off him.

I fought my way to the doors. Outside, the rain was pelting down. But in the distance I could see flashing blue lights coming along the road from Stembridge, and soon I could hear the sirens. There was the sound of an engine being driven at top speed, a

squeal of brakes . . . and a terrible
crash.

I ran down the drive and stopped
by the gates. A car had smashed into
a tree, at almost exactly the same spot
where Reverend Holmes had spotted
Smith and Wesson. It was a total
wreck. Police cars surrounded it, and
I was just in time to see Walters being
dragged clear. Then I saw whose car
it was.

That's two shocks for Mr Pinkerton in one night, I thought . . .

Three days later I was standing on the drive once more with Richard and the other kids. The sun was shining, and we were waiting for the coach to take us home. I was reading the latest edition of *The Stembridge Gazette*. It was mostly about me.

'Schoolgirl Solves Mystery, Finds Missing Loot,' said the headline. And that more or less summed it up. Walters hadn't been badly hurt in the crash, and was now safely in police custody. And because of my genius as a detective, the other Lucky Number Bandit had been caught as well.

I had realized Edward Courtenay and the local burglar were one and the same person. It had made perfect sense.

We'd used the map to find him. As I'd suspected, he was in the cave, surrounded by heaps of money which he'd forgotten how to spend. He didn't give us any trouble. The police took him to hospital, where they soon discovered he'd lost most of his memory as a result of that blow on the head.

When he'd come round, he'd been so confused he'd thought he was back in the Amazon jungle. Somehow he had made his way to the cave, where he'd been living ever since, surviving with the skills he'd learned as an adventurer. The only other thing he'd remembered was how to steal. Hence the disappearing food.

The doctors said he'd recover, although then he'd have to stand trial for his crimes. Strangely enough, his parents were quite happy. At least they knew he was alive, I suppose. Maybe things would work out for them when he got out of jail. I hoped so.

Lots of other people were happy, too, I thought as the coach arrived. Richard had won a five-pound book token for the best project, which was about what I'd expected from stingy Mr Pinkerton. But Richard was happy with that. And Mrs Sternwood was happy because Mr Pinkerton would have to travel back on the coach. That meant her seat was taken, so she was going home by train. Alone.

And there was one thing which made everyone feel *very* relieved. Greenstreet's feet didn't smell any more.

'Look out, Sam,' said Richard as Greenstreet came over.

'It's OK, Richard,' I said. 'Everything's under control.'

'Is there anything I can do for you, Sam?' said Greenstreet.

'How nice of you to offer, Steven,' I said, smiling. 'You *could* carry my stuff over to the coach, I suppose . . .'

Greenstreet smiled back, and scurried off with my rucksack and sleeping bag to the mob round the driver and Mr Pinkerton.

'But . . . but you two are deadly enemies,' said Richard, bewildered. 'I don't get it. Are you ill?'

'No, Richard,' I said, and smiled. 'Let's just say Steven and I have er . . . signed a peace treaty.'

That wasn't strictly true. Things

were going to be different between us, but that was because I'd realized Greenstreet's zip-up bag contained . . . a teddy bear. Lady Jennifer had planted the idea in my brain by talking about her son and *his* teddy. I'd confronted Greenstreet and he'd confessed.

He'd also begged me not to tell anyone. I'd agreed, but on condition that he throw away his trainers, wash his feet, and borrow a pair of shoes until he got home. Oh yes, and I said he'd have to be nice to me from now on. I knew it wouldn't last for ever, but I was going to have fun while it did.

Then a large hand landed on my shoulder, and all thoughts of fun vanished from my mind. I turned round . . . and found myself looking into a pair of twinkly blue eyes.

'Oh, hello, Sarge . . .' I said, my heart sinking.

I'd had a lecture from Mrs Sternwood about getting involved in things I shouldn't, of course, and Mr

Pinkerton had given me a real telling off about sliding down those bannisters. Othewise I'd come out of this caper as a heroine.

And in all the chaos, no-one had asked me what I'd been doing inside Courtenay House at midnight. That was the sort of question I'd expect from Sergeant Cuff. But I got away with it.

'Don't worry, Sam,' he said with a smile. 'I've just come to say goodbye . . . *and* to make sure you get on that coach.'

'I'm going, I'm going,' I said. 'This place is too dangerous for a sweet, innocent little schoolgirl like me . . .'

Besides, I hated to admit it, but I *was* actually quite looking forward to seeing my family again. Even my big brother.

Hey, I thought. Maybe I *am* ill, after all . . .

THE END

A SELECTED LIST OF TITLES
AVAILABLE FROM YEARLING BOOKS

THE PRICES SHOWN BELOW WERE CORRECT AT THE TIME OF GOING TO PRESS. HOWEVER TRANSWORLD PUBLISHERS RESERVE THE RIGHT TO SHOW NEW RETAIL PRICES ON COVERS WHICH MAY DIFFER FROM THOSE PREVIOUSLY ADVERTISED IN THE TEXT OR ELSEWHERE.

All Corgi/Bantam Books are available at your bookshop or newsagent, or can be ordered from the following address:
Transworld Publishers Ltd,
Cash Sales Department,
P.O. Box 11, Falmouth, Cornwall TR10 9EN

Please send a cheque or postal order (no currency) and allow £1.00 for postage and packing for the first book plus 30p for each subsequent book ordered to a maximum charge of £3.00 if ordering seven or more books.

Overseas customers, including Eire, please allow £2.00 for postage and packing for the first book, £1.00 for the second book, and an additional 50p for each subsequent title ordered.

NAME (Block Letters)...

ADDRESS ....

....

We hope you enjoyed reading this book. If you would like to receive details of the latest new children's books published by Transworld Publishers, please send your name and address to: The Children's Books Editor, Transworld Publishers Ltd, 61-63 Uxbridge Road, Ealing, London W5 5SA, marking your envelope CHILDREN'S NEWSLETTER.